Hooked by the BBC 4

Naughty Desires

The final Book 4 in the *Hooked by the BBC Series*

Amber Carden

CHAPTER ONE: Reawakened Desires 1

CHAPTER TWO: Strange Loyalty 10

CHAPTER THREE: Revelations 19

CHAPTER FOUR: Rekindling the Thrill 29

CHAPTER FIVE: Rekindling the Thrill 39

CHAPTER SIX: The Orgy 49

CHAPTER ONE:
Reawakened Desires

Sam could feel her stomach tightening as she watched the screen in front of the both of them, the video playing in slow motion. Tyrell has recorded them and she had no idea. She looked at Mike who was still watching and rewinding the tape, unsure of what to say.

Eventually, he paused the video and turned to look at her? "How long has this been going on?" he asked, his voice coming out a little choked. "How long were you planning on keeping this from me?"

"Look, I can explain." Sam started, swallowing slightly. "I can explain, I wasn't trying to hide it. I just knew that I had to do this for you and Tyrell gave me this proposal that if I slept with him he would wipe your debt clean."

"That's not how shit like this work Sam." Mike said, raising his voice slightly. "You don't make deals with the devil, you only end up burned. Tyrell just wanted to hit and quit, I doubt that he had any intentions of letting me go."

"Well what choice did I have? You're the one who got involved with a drug dealer yet you're giving me problems trying to fix the issue you made?"

"Oh, that's what you're using to make yourself feel better? You did this for me? I don't buy it. I think you're just horny for some BBC again."

"Excuse me?!" Sam shouted, getting to her feet. "Where do you get off talking to me like that?"

Mike bit his lip, regretting his words. He was annoyed, yes but that wasn't a reason to throw shade at her lifestyle. After all, wasn't he involved in it as well? He didn't know how to feel though, the thought of her sleeping with someone else was one thing but did that person have to be his boss? And he knew Tyrell well enough to know that even if she did what he said, the likelihood of him being free was very low.

Mike sighed and sat down on the bed, burying his hands in his hands. "I appreciate what you were trying to do and I'm sorry for putting us in this situation. I'm just worried about you getting involved with Tyrell, that's all."

Sam took a seat besides her husband. "I understand what you mean but maybe we can hope for the best? You always say that Tyrell is a man of his words."

"He is but I also know that he likes to screw people over and apparently he has a thing for screwing my wife now. This just doesn't feel like a solution, if anything it feels like we're only digging ourselves deeper."

"So what do we do?" Sam asked.

"I think you need to tell him that it's over, Sam." His tone was softer now, like he was pleasing with her. "If this was really for me then you're done now. So we can move on."

"Is it really that easy?" Sam asked, reaching for her phone where Tyrell's contact information was stored.

"I don't know, but there's only one way to find out."

Sam sighed and looked at her phone. She wanted to listen to her husband, she really did but what would that mean for her and what she wanted? Yes, she did this for him but she couldn't deny how good it felt to be with Tyrell. He dominated her, pounded her over and over until she felt like she couldn't take it anymore. He was a bad guy no doubt but why did he have to fuck so good?

"I guess I have no choice." She says, opening her phone up and heading to her messages to draft a text to send to Tyrell.

Just at that moment, her phone made a buzzing noise, interrupting the silence of the room. Sam felt her heart drop as she saw the message, it was from Tyrell.

"Tomorrow night. My place. We aren't done yet."

Her hand tightened around the phone. The words were simple enough but she could hear his voice behind them, commanding and authoritative. She knew what he was capable of and she knew exactly what he wanted. Could she resist?

"Who is it?" Mike's voice cut through her thoughts but she quickly put the phone away, hoping her guilt didn't show on her face.

"No one," she replied, avoiding his gaze.

Mike sighed, his expression weary. "Sam, if you want to keep our marriage together, you need to stop this. Whatever thrill you're getting out of this, I can't do it. I'm asking you. End it with him...for good."

She nodded, forcing a smile to put him at ease. "I will. I promise."

But as she lay in bed that night, staring up at the ceiling, she couldn't help but think about Tyrell's message. *'We're not done yet'.*

She thought back to when last they hooked up and the way he had made her feel. She hadn't felt anything like that in a very long time and as she drifted off to sleep, only one thought was on her mind.

Tyrell wasn't done with her and she wasn't done with him either.

The next day, Sam pretended to oversleep and waited for her husband to leave the house before she got up to start getting ready to go meet Tyrell. She waited in silence, listening for the faint sound of the garage door closing. As soon as she heard Mike's car pull out of the driveway, she quickly grabbed her coat and purse, slipping out the door and into her car before she could talk herself out of it. She knew she should be staying home and honoring her promise to Mike but all she could think about was being under Tyrell again.

A couple of minutes later, she was in front of Tyrell's building, guarded by hidden security with the sharpest eyes. One of them nodded and escorts her in, barely speaking as they led her up to Tyrell's apartment. The suite was just as lavish as she remembere, sleek leather, floor-to-ceiling windows and artwork that must have cost more than her entire house.

They leave her alone in a waiting area, offering nothing more than a curt nod to her. She glances around the room and it was then she realized that she had no control over this situation or any power over it either.

Minutes later, she heard footsteps and turned just as Tyrell entered. He looked as composed as ever, in his tailored suit.

"Sam," he greeted her, a smirk tugging at the corner of his mouth. "Right on time."

She straightened, immediately getting to the point. "You sent that video to Mike without my consent," she said, keeping her voice as steady as she could. "Why would you do that?"

Tyrell's smirk widened,. "Why do you care?" he asked, his voice smooth and unbothered, as if her question barely registered to him.

"Because it's... it's not okay," she stammered, finding her confidence slipping under his gaze. "I thought this was supposed to be between us, I was doing that to help my husband out but then sending it to him, that wasn't part of the deal."

Tyrell laughed. "The deal? You still think this is about what you want?"

Sam's mouth opened and she began making a staggering defense on why what he did wasn't okay. Tyrell didn't give her the chance to get into it though, before she knew what was happening, he unbuckled his pants, crossed the room, slipped his dick out and shoved it into her mouth before she could protest.

He gripped her chin, tilting her face towards him as he used the head to trace the corner of her lips then shove back into her mouth again.

"Let's get one thing straight," he said as his fingers held her jaw in place. "I didn't call you here to talk about what you want, Sam."

All she could taste was the strong, musky flavor of him. He held on to her jaw, guiding her head up and dow his shaft when he noticed that she was making no effort to suck on him by herself.

"Now," Tyrell continued. "Why don't you show me that you understand."

Sam sat there, his cock in between her lips, feeling both humiliated and aroused. She used her tongue to tentatively lick the head and flushed with warmth when she saw Tyrell close his eyes slightly with pleasure.

He may have most of the control here but she still had some tricks to take the power back. She reached out to him and grabbed the shaft, stroking it gently as she made a sucking motion with her lips.

"Good girl," he murmured. He stepped back, turning toward the hall, gesturing for her to follow him into his bedroom. Now she knew this was a dangerous game but still she followed Tyrell down the dimly lit hall and into his bedroom.

"Let's see if you remember why you're here," he said, taking off the rest of his clothes.

There was no turning back now.

CHAPTER TWO:
Strange Loyalty

Tyrell stood in front of her, completely naked and with his dick erect, calling her to him. Sam could see it pulsing, the top of the head glistening with precum, precum that she feels an intense urge to lick off.

She lifted her head up to look at him but found that she was unable to hold his gaze. He was staring at her intensely, in a way that almost made her breathless.

"On your knees," he commanded her, pointing his fingers downward to indicate that he wanted her in front of his dick.

Sam's heart was pounding hard as she dropped down in front of Tyrell, feeling the cold floor beneath her knees. She kept her face down but then he tilted her face up, telling her to "Look at me." he ordered.

He held onto his dick and brought it in front of her face once again, tapping her lips with it slightly. "Open," he ordered and Sam obeyed, parting her lips as he leaned forward and slid his dick between her lips with a deliberate slowness that caused him to groan out loud.

She closed her lips around it, feeling the precum on the tip of her tongue. Tyrell let out a small gasp then smirked. "Show me, I want to see just how much you enjoy this."

Sam began to suck gently at first then swirled her tongue around it, pressing her lips tightly around the piece of candy. More precum began to leak out of it and this caused her to increase the intensity of her movement. She wanted to see Tyrell begging in front of her, lost in the pleasure that she was giving him.

"Good girl," he groaned, titling his head back as he savored what she did to him.

She sucked his cock a bit deeper into her mouth, tilting her head back just slightly, letting him see the way she worked her mouth around it. He let out a long, strained groan as he shoved it into her mouth, hitting the back of her throat.

"Don't stop," he whispered, thrusting it into her mouth over and over again. "That's right, take your time. Don't stop."

Sam's cheeks were burning at this point but she obeyed, letting her tongue trace along the shaft as she sucked on. Tyrell was thrusting faster now and she was finding it hard to keep up. He grabbed her head, gripping her hair and shoving his dick deeper into her mouth, causing her to gag on it.

She ran her tongue along the head of his dick and Tyrell let out a long, strained groan as he shoved his dick into her mouth one last time, spraying the back of her throat with his cum.

"Fuckkkk," he groaned. "Take my cum, white bitch." He said, stroking his dick into her mouth slowly as he came in it.

"See?" he murmured, "I knew you could be... do it."

Sam swallowed his cum, his dick still in her mouth. She wasn't sure what she liked most about this interaction, whether it was the control that he held over

"Good," he said. "Now that I've seen you follow directions, let's see how you handle the rest."

With one last, lingering look, he took his dick out of her mouth, now soft and still dripping a little bit of cum.

He released her from his grip, stepping back just enough to observe her as she straightened. She could tell by his expression that she'd pleased him. Tyrell reached down, taking her by the hand and pulling her up to her feet. Without a word, he led her toward the bed. She followed him, her heart racing as he held onto her hand.

When they reached the edge of the bed, he stopped, turning to face her. He placed his hands on her shoulders, guiding her backward until she felt the mattress behind her. He straddled her, then slowly started taking off all her clothes until she was left in nothing but her bra.

"Pink lace...and you were acting like you didn't want this." He said, chuckling.

"You came here to satisfy me," he said. "And I'm not done with you yet."

He leaned into her, his hands trailing down her side as he felt up her body. She held her breath as she felt his touch tracing over her skin. He leaned down and brushed his lips against her neck. His hands gripped her waist tight and she arched underneath him, as he got between her thighs and buried himself into her.

"Tell me you want this," he whispered, sighing as he thrusted into her slowly.

"I... I want this," she replied, as his thrusts sent wave after wave of pleasure into her.

"Good," he said. "Now, let's see if you can keep up."

Tyrell increased the intensity of his thrusts, driving himself into Sam until she was absolutely breathless. He wrapped her legs around him, which caused him to go deeper into her.

The sound of their bodies slapping against each other filled the room. Sam was so wet that he couldn't resist leaning over and pounding into her repeatedly. Sam could feel her pulse quickening as he gripped unto her. He leaned down and brushed his lips against her neck and she let out a shaky breath, unable to hide her reaction as his mouth found her most sensitive spot under her ear.

A low hum of satisfaction came from his throat when he felt her tremble beneath him, his fingers pressing firmly into her hips. He buries his hands into her hair, pulling her head back just enough to expose her neck as he moved writhing her deeper, his thrusts more relentless.

"You can take it, can't you?" he taunted, his voice a low growl.

"Yes," she gasped, barely able to form any words as he drove her to the edge. She couldn't think any coherent thoughts, all that was in her mind was how good he was making her feel.

He smirked to himself when he noticed the effect he was having on her. It was enough to drive him over the edge and it did. Sam could feel him shuddering as he got closer and closer, his grip on her tightening and his breaths becoming more shallow until he couldn't take it anymore and he pulled out quickly, cumming all over the mattress.

Before he had let her cum before he did, this time it was all about him. It was like he was trying to send Sam a message, a message that said 'he held all the cards, not her.'

He let out a satisfied sigh then headed to the en-suite bathroom not too far from the bed. He came out and threw a towel her way to clean herself up with. She took it with thanks but could only lay there to catch her breath, her body still buzzing from the aftershocks.

She sat up then smoothed the towel all over herself. She didn't know if she was trying to erase the evidence of what just happened so Mike would be none the wiser when she got back home. She looked in Tyrell's direction, watching as he relieved against the pillows, his dick soft by this point.

When she was finally able to steady her breathing, she mustered up the courage to ask the question that had been lingering at the back of her mind. "So after this, does this mean that we're done? Does this mean that Mike's debt is clear? Am I free to go? I'm not sure how long I can keep doing this."

Tyrell has a smirk on his face and he took a deep breath before he answered. "Done?" He repeated the word as if he were tasting it. Sam swallowed, unsure of what his response would be. It was so hard to predict this man.

Tyrell leaned forward, his eyes narrowing as he looked her over. "You'll be done, Sam," he began, "when I decide I've had enough. When I'm ready to let you go, and not a moment before."

A chill ran down her spine at that moment and she could feel anxiety rising in her chest. Her husband had been right, nothing she did would fix this problem. Tyrell would just keep using her and using her until he got tired of her. How foolish of her to believe that she had anything valuable to offer this man that would make him forget the fact that Mike owed him thousands of dollars.

Her fingers tightened around the towel as she fought to maintain her composure. "I thought we had a deal," she murmured, her voice faint yet hoping that he might reconsider.

He tilted his head, a slight smile on his lips as he watched her struggle to assert herself. "We do, Sam. And I intend to keep my end of it. But remember, you came to me. You wanted this arrangement, and now you'll finish it on my terms."

Sam swallowed, she wanted to protest but he was right. She wanted this and she got exactly what she was looking for.

CHAPTER THREE:
Revelations

Mike was at the kitchen table, fingers clenched around his phone as the video loaded. He didn't know what to expect when the anonymous message pinged onto his screen. His gut told him it was another recording from Tyrell, another twisted reminder that he still wasn't free from the man's control, that Tyrell still had Sam wrapped around his finger but he couldn't be sure. Not until he opened it.

The video started to play and Mike's breath caught as he saw Sam, his wife, kneeling in front of Tyrell and sucking on his dick. Her face was turned toward the camera, although she was clearly oblivious to its presence. He watched, anger and shame burning through him as Tyrell's hands roamed over her, grabbing her hair, claiming her, treating her as if she were his.

"Damn it," he muttered under his breath, hitting pause but unable to look away. Why was Tyrell doing this? Why send these to him, was it just a power play, a way to show Mike who was really in control?

The sound of Sam's laughter drifted through from the other room, and Mike felt his anger twist into confusion. She had promised him she'd end things, that this entire arrangement was over. Yet here she was, caught on camera again, in Tyrell's bed.

When he confronted her last time, she'd looked at him with wide, guilt-ridden eyes, "It was for you," she'd told him, voice trembling. "I only did it to protect you."

And he'd believed her. At least, he had wanted to believe her. But seeing her like this, caught on video made him doubt everything.

He heard footsteps approaching and quickly locked his phone, shoving it into his pocket just as Sam walked into the kitchen. She smiled at him, reaching for a coffee mug, her face calm and almost carefree. It was as if she had no idea what he'd just seen.

"Morning," she said, pouring coffee and leaning against the counter. "You're up early."

Mike's gaze became sharp all of a sudden. He couldn't keep the suspicion from his face. "Couldn't sleep," he muttered, the edge in his tone unmistakable. He watched her carefully, looking for any hint of guilt, any sign that she knew what he had just seen.

Sam took a sip of her coffee, glancing at him over the rim of her mug. "Are you all right?" she asked, her brow creasing slightly.

"Just... got a lot on my mind." He forced himself to look away. He hated this feeling, it's as if Tyrell had invaded their lives, placing a wedge between him and Sam that he couldn't remove. And it was all his fault.

"I was thinking," he began carefully, trying to keep his voice steady, "about what you said... that you'd stopped everything with Tyrell."

Sam's face got tight, her eyes darting away for a fraction of a second. It was so subtle but Mike caught it.

"Of course I did," she replied, her voice defensive. "You know that."

"Right," he replied, barely able to keep the bitterness from his voice. "So if he... I don't know, tried to reach out to you again, you'd tell me. Right?"

She looked at him, a little too quickly, her smile tight. "Yes, Mike. I would tell you."

The lie twisted in his chest, making it hard to breathe. He wasn't sure if he wanted to call her out on it now, to ask her outright why she was still sneaking around or if he wanted to let it slide, to keep the peace a little longer.

But then his phone buzzed again in his pocket, the vibration cutting through the silence between them. He didn't pull it out, he didn't have to. He already knew what it would be.

Sam looked at him, brow furrowing. "You going to get that?"

He shook his head. "No. It can wait."

She nodded, though he could see the question in her eyes. But she didn't press him and a part of him was grateful for that. He wasn't sure he could keep it together if she did.

As she left the room, he pulled out his phone, his hands shaking slightly as he checked the notification. Another video, just like before. Another message from Tyrell, taunting him with the knowledge that Sam was still under his thumb.

He pressed play again, his heart pounding as he watched the scene unfold. Part of him couldn't look away. Part of him was drawn in, watching Tyrell take control of Sam, watching the way she responded, the way she surrendered.

And in that moment, Mike realized he wasn't sure what angered him more, the fact that Sam was lying to him or the fact that some dark part of him couldn't help but watch.

Mike stood there with his phone tightly gripped in his hands. All he could do was glare at the screen as he watched this man thrust into his wife over and over again.

As the video continued, Tyrell's hands moved over Sam and he watched his wife's face flush with pleasure, her body responding openly. She looked lost in the moment, by the way Tyrell touched her. And while Mike wanted to look away, he knew that his body wanted him to keep watching.

"What am I doing?" he muttered to himself as his eyes followed Tyrell's movements, his grip on Sam. It was different, so different from how Mike would touch her. Where Mike was gentle with Sam, not wanting to hurt her. Tyrell took whatever he wanted without caring how she felt.

Somehow knowing that there was a side to his wife that he didn't know who to bring out made a wave of heat pass through him and his pulse quickened even as Tyrell increased the speed of his thrusts.

The conflicting emotions in his chest seemed to fight to be the dominant feeling, his anger fading as he realized he was... excited. In ways he hadn't felt in a long time since well Jay.

Glancing around the room to make sure Sam wasn't nearby, he quietly snuck down the hallway, slipping into the guest bathroom and locking the door behind him. His fingers shook slightly as he set his phone on the counter, leaning over the sink and staring down at the screen, the heat in his dick intensifying.

"Damn it," he muttered, feeling shame mix with the rush of arousal. He pressed play again and he buried his hand into his pants, pulling his dick out. It was red, erect and already leaking precum. He pressed play again and began stroking his penis in rhythm with the way Tyrell was pounding into Sam. His breathing became shallow, almost like his hand was moving on its own.

The sound of Sam's moans filled his mind, she was moaning in a way that she had never with him. It made him feel so turned on somehow, the emasculation of it all.

As he gave in to the need, the images of Sam's face, her body arching under Tyrell's touch, filled his mind, and the intensity of his response shocked him. His dick jerked as he stroked it harder and harder, practically turning red from all the friction. The pleasure grew, overtaking him, building quickly as he lost himself in the sounds, the sight and everything.

Pretty soon he felt a tightening in his stomach and pleasure washed over him as he came into the sink. He let out a quiet sigh, not wanting Sam to hear what was going on.

He stood there for a moment, eyes closed, catching breath. He rested his hands on the sink as he struggled to pull himself back from the edge. He glanced down at the phone, still paused on the video, and felt his stomach twist again but not from pleasure this time.

"What's wrong with me?" he whispered, shaking his head. He couldn't believe he'd given in to that impulse, couldn't believe that something like this had gotten to him so deeply. The shame settled heavily in his chest, mixing with the frustration he was feeling.

He shut off the phone, the silence of the room even louder now that the video was gone. As he leaned over the sink, he could still see her face in his mind and he hated himself a little for it.

The thought of facing Sam now...she had no idea that he'd received the videos or how they affected him and he wasn't sure he wanted her to know.

Running a hand through his hair, he took a deep breath. He knew that eventually he'd have to confront her about this whole thing but then he began to think, did he have to? Couldn't he just let the sleeping dogs lie?

And besides for whatever misguided reason, his wife was doing this for him. He never would have been in this mess if he hadn't gotten involved with the wrong crowd. So can he really blame his wife for looking after him especially after he kept things from her in that way.

He splashed cold water on his face and it grounded him. He would have to confront all of these emotions much later, right now he could just be grateful he wasn't in anymore danger.

CHAPTER FOUR:
Rekindling the Thrill

Sam's hands shook as she stared at the message on her husband's phone. She couldn't believe it, Tyrell was doing it again. He sent videos of them to Mike's phone again!

She knew he did this before but why would he do it again? What was he gaining out of it? Why did he keep doing this? She felt exposed and betrayed again but what could she expect from a drug dealer? She couldn't let this keep happening, she had to put a stop to it right now.

It didn't take long for her to find herself back at Tyrell's lavish mansion. The guards let her in without a word, clearly used to her by now but Sam stormed past them without a glance, driven by anger and anxiety. Tyrell was seated on a sleek leather couch in the waiting area, his attention seemingly elsewhere as she entered but then a faint smirk curled on his lips as he looked up and met her staring at him.

"Back so soon?" he drawled, amusement in his eyes. "Didn't expect to see you again so quickly."

Sam clenched her fists, barely holding back her anger. "What are you doing, Tyrell?" she demanded. "Sending those videos to Mike? Again? That's not fair. You're crossing a line and you know it."

He chuckled, leaning back against the couch with a casualness that only made her more frustrated. "Fair?" he repeated, arching a brow. "Sam, we're far past fair here. I don't owe you or Mike anything. I've been more than generous, given everything he owes me."

"But this is different," she shot back, her voice filled with desperation. "This is personal. You're deliberately trying to humiliate him, humiliate me."

Tyrell's smirk only deepened. "Maybe," he said smoothly. "Or maybe I'm just reminding him of the cost of his choices. Besides, you weren't complaining before. You seemed pretty eager to come back every time."

Sam's face flushed with embarrassment and anger. "That's not the point, Tyrell," she said quietly, her voice shaking slightly. "This, this isn't ethical. What you're doing, it's manipulative."

He shrugged, unbothered by her accusation. "Ethics are for people who don't hold all the cards. But," he continued, tilting his head as if considering her, "I'm feeling generous today. Maybe I'll wipe Mike's debt and we can call it even."

All of Mike's debt, gone? She should have felt relieved, grateful even. This was the end of their troubles, the escape they'd been waiting for. But then reality sank in, she felt disappointment. If Tyrell cleared the debt, then... this strange, reckless arrangement with him would end.

Seeing her hesitate, Tyrell's smile grew. "What's wrong, Sam? Not the reaction I was expecting. Shouldn't you be grateful?"

She forced herself to look away, trying to gather her thoughts. "Of course I'm grateful," she replied. "It's just... a lot to process." She thought of Mike, the relief he'd feel if he knew Tyrell's threats were finally over. He'd been so anxious, so weighed down by the debt and now he could breathe easy. She knew that was what mattered most, but somehow, the finality of it left her feeling unsettled.

"Take it or leave it," Tyrell said coolly, watching her closely. "I'm not offering again."

Sam swallowed, fighting the strange pang in her chest. She nodded, forcing herself to focus on what this meant for her family. "Fine. We'll take it," she replied. "Just stop sending those videos. You've done enough."

Tyrell raised his hands in a mock gesture of surrender. "Consider it done." He leaned forward. "But let's be clear, Sam, this doesn't mean I'm done with you. I let you go when I decide to. Understood?"

Sam met his gaze. "As long as Mike's debt is cleared, that's all that matters to me." She turned to leave, feeling the weight of his eyes on her back but she kept her head high, refusing to let him see her uncertainty.

Back home, she told Mike the news and he stared at her, stunned. "All of it?" he repeated, his voice filled with disbelief and relief. "We're... we're finally free of him?"

"Yes," Sam replied, forcing a smile. "It's over."

He exhaled, closing his eyes as if a massive weight had just lifted from his shoulders. "This is it, Sam. We can finally move on."

She nodded, willing herself to feel the same relief he felt but then there was an odd emptiness in her. She pushed it aside, knowing that Mike needed his peace about this more than anything. For him, this was a fresh start. She just had to let go of everything and believe that too.

She lay in bed that night, staring up at the ceiling, her mind restless despite the late hour. Tyrell's decision to end things had left her feeling conflicted. Part of her had been relieved when he'd offered to clear Mike's debt, thinking this would finally bring peace. Yet she couldn't shake the emptiness in her chest.

Tyrell had brought her so much pleasure. Could she really give all of that up?

Beside her, Mike stirred, glancing over and noticing the distant look on her face. "You okay?" he asked,

Sam hesitated, wondering how to even begin explaining this. "Yeah... I guess." She turned onto her side, facing him. "It's just... I don't know. Everything feels different now. Going back to normal just seems strange."

He sighed, reaching over to brush a strand of hair from her face. "Look, Sam, we've been through a lot. Maybe it'll just take some time to get used to things being... simple again."

She bit her lip, hesitating. "It's not just that. I mean, after everything, it's hard to pretend things haven't changed. Tyrell... he showed me something I didn't even realize I wanted. Or needed. I don't think I can just go back to how things were before."

She paused, gathering her thoughts. "It's like, now that I've... experienced that, I don't know if I can settle back into what we had."

Mike was quiet, his brow furrowed as he processed her words. "Are you saying..." He cleared his throat, glancing away briefly before meeting her gaze again. "You're saying you want more of... that? Even if it's not with him? That dangerous kind of toxic sex?"

She nodded slowly. "Yeah something like that. We've ended things with all these other people and I just know I'm not ready to go back to normal now.."

Mike exhaled, rubbing the back of his neck. "I get it, Sam. Really, I do. And as much as it's tough for me to admit, I know things changed for both of us." He looked back at her, his expression softer now. "Maybe we don't have to go back to the way things were. Maybe we don't have to give up on this lifestlye now that Tyrell is gone."

Sam looked at him, surprised. "You mean...?"

He shrugged, a small smile tugging at his lips. "We tried it before, right? With Jay, Andre. And I'll admit, there was something kind of... exciting about it. Maybe we could look online again, see if we can find someone who fits what you're looking for. Together."

Sam's pulse quickened at the suggestion, a thrill running through her at the thought. "You'd really be okay with that?"

He chuckled, shaking his head slightly. "Okay might be pushing it, I'm still recovering from the whole Tyrell thing but I liked parts of it when we did it last time. And I want to make you happy and if this is part of it, I think I can get there. As long as we're doing it together."

She smiled, feeling a warmth spread through her. "Okay, then. Let's... let's give it a try."

Over the next few days, they set up dusted off their laptop and reactivated their dormant profiles together, crafting a message that felt genuine but also hinted at their interests. It was so strange being back here, scrolling through profiles and mooming for couples that shared the same open-minded as they did. They laughed, hesitated, and debated over potential matches, the whole experience bringing a lightheartedness she hadn't felt in a long time with her husband. It was nice, feeling completely different from all the drama Tyrell brought.

Finally, they received a message from a couple that caught their attention. The profile showed a couple named Erin and Jamal, both in their early thirties, a lot younger than Mike and Sam. They seemed to have an easygoing, adventurous vibe and were an interracial couple, just like Andre and his wife.

Their message was warm and inviting, expressing a mutual interest and excitement in meeting.

Mike raised his eyebrows as he read the message aloud. "They're asking if we want to meet up for drinks this weekend." He glanced at Sam, a faint grin playing on his lips. "What do you think?"

"I think… I think we should go for it."

They messaged Erin and Jamal back, arranging a casual meetup at a local bar that coming Friday. When the day arrived, Sam found herself feeling both nervous and excited, choosing an outfit that was just suggestive enough, wanting to feel attractive and confident. Mike gave her an encouraging smile as they left the house, his hand resting reassuringly on her back as they made their way to the bar.

CHAPTER FIVE:
Rekindling the Thrill

Sam adjusted her dress nervously as she and Mike walked into the dimly lit bar. Her heart was pounding, excitement and nerves rushing through her. This would be the first time that since Andre that they would be getting involved with another couple that they had only spoken with online. She could only hope that this would go better than that time.

Erin and Jamal were already there, seated at a cozy booth near the back. Erin greeted them with a warm smile, her blonde curls bouncing as she waved them over, while Jamal extended a hand in greeting, Mike catching it first.

"Hey, you must be Sam and Mike!" Erin greeted them, sliding out of the booth to shake their hands. She was petite and energetic, with a welcoming smile, blonde hair and a natural warmth that made Sam feel instantly comfortable. Her partner, Jamal, stood up next to her, tall and broad-shouldered with an effortless charm about him. He had a fade and a relaxed, charismatic energy that Sam couldn't help but notice right away.

"Nice to finally meet you both," Jamal said, shaking Mike's hand firmly and then Sam's. His smile was easygoing, the kind that instantly put people at ease. "We've been looking forward to this."

They all settled into the booth, Mike and Sam sitting across from Erin and Jamal. A waitress came by, taking their drink orders, Sam opted for a glass of wine, while Mike ordered a beer. She noticed that Erin and Jamal were both sipping cocktails, looking completely at ease as they leaned back and smiled at them.

"So, how are you both feeling?" Erin asked with a grin, breaking the ice. "Nervous? Excited?"

Sam laughed. "A bit of both, to be honest," she admitted. "It's nothing new to us but we've been out of the game for a while if we're being honest."

Jamal chuckled. "You're not alone there. It took us a while to figure out what we were both comfortable with and that caused us to take a lot of breaks but now it's something we both enjoy. There's really no pressure, we're just here to see if there's a connection and have a good time."

Erin nodded, reaching over to give Jamal's hand a gentle squeeze. "It's all about having fun, you know? We want you both to feel at ease. This isn't about expectations or anything, it's just a chance to get to know each other."

Sam appreciated how straightforward they were. It felt refreshing, like she didn't have to hide her curiosity or excitement. She exchanged a glance with Mike, who gave her a reassuring smile before turning to Erin and Jamal.

"So, you guys have done this a few times, I take it?" Mike asked, sounding genuinely curious.

Erin nodded, laughing lightly. "Yeah, we have a bit of experience with it. Honestly, it's been a fun way for us to explore things together while keeping our own boundaries clear."

Sam took a sip of her wine. "What kind of boundaries, if you don't mind me asking?"

"Oh, not at all," Erin replied easily. "For me, I like to watch more than anything. Jamal... well, he's the one who usually gets involved, and I love seeing him enjoy himself." She glanced at Jamal with a playful smile and he chuckled, reaching over to give her hand a squeeze.

Jamal leaned in a bit, his gaze resting on Sam with a subtle spark of interest. "And what about you two? What drew you to this?"

Sam hesitated, glancing at Mike. They'd talked about this, of course, but putting it into words still felt strange. "Well... we've been through a lot this past year," she began, choosing her words carefully. "There were some... situations that opened our eyes to different things we didn't know we might like. And we thought... why not try something new together?"

Mike nodded, chiming in. "Yeah, it was kind of unexpected but we realized it brought us closer in some ways. We're just... exploring, I guess."

Erin smiled, nodding as if she understood completely. "It sounds like you two are on the same page. That's the most important thing."

Sam felt herself relaxing more and more, the initial nerves replaced by a genuine interest in Erin and Jamal's experiences. She found herself drawn to Jamal's easygoing charm, his looks and how authentic he was with Erin. She could see why Erin was so supportive of his role in their dynamic, his confidence was magnetic, almost impossible to resist.

At one point, Jamal leaned in, his gaze lingering on Sam. "So, Sam," he said with a playful grin. "What do you think so far? Not too intimidating, I hope?"

She laughed, feeling a faint blush creep up her cheeks. "Not at all," she replied honestly. "Actually, it's... nice. I feel like we're all just here to enjoy each other's company."

Erin nodded in agreement, her eyes twinkling with amusement. "Exactly. That's the whole point. Just good company, good conversation, and seeing where things go."

Mike chuckled, giving Sam's hand a gentle squeeze under the table. She glanced at him, he seemed at ease too, and she could tell he was enjoying the atmosphere.

"So," Sam ventured, "I noticed that you, Erin, mentioned you like to watch Jamal rather than join in. Is that... just a preference?"

Erin smiled, glancing over at Jamal. "Yeah, it's definitely a preference. But there's more to it than that." She shoved Jamal in the sides, as if encouraging him to explain further.

Jamal cleared his throat, looking directly at Sam and Mike with an easy smile. "You could say it's partly because there are... certain things I enjoy that Erin isn't really into. It's actually why this works so well for us."

Sam tilted her head, curiosity piqued. "What do you mean?"

"Well," Erin began, looking to Jamal to see if he wanted to elaborate. "He has, let's say... certain tastes."

Sam furrowed her brow, glancing between them, unsure what they were getting at. "Tastes? Like... preferences?"

Jamal nodded, a slight grin playing at the corner of his mouth. "Yeah, I guess you could say that. I'm into... light BDSM."

"BDSM?" Sam repeated, blinking as she tried to process what he'd just said. She wasn't sure what she had expected but that word caught her off guard. Her cheeks warmed slightly, and she looked to Mike, who seemed equally intrigued, though not exactly surprised. Turning back to Jamal, she managed, "Oh. I see."

But truthfully, she didn't see. Sam wasn't sure how she felt about it. BDSM wasn't something she'd ever imagined herself exploring. To her, it seemed so extreme. Just the thought of it made her feel slightly uncomfortable, even a bit nervous.

Sensing her hesitation, Jamal gave her an understanding nod. "It's not for everyone, I know," he said. "It's something Erin and I are really open about and it's also why she prefers to watch rather than participate. It's just not her thing, and that's totally fine."

Erin nodded, adding, "Exactly. I love seeing him happy, and this arrangement lets us both enjoy ourselves in our own way."

Sam fidgeted slightly. The thought of engaging with something so outside her comfort zone made her want to retreat. She turned to Mike, meeting his gaze with a look that said, 'I'm not sure about this.'

Sensing her discomfort, Mike placed a reassuring hand on her back. "We don't have to do anything we're not comfortable with, Sam," he said gently. "It's all up to us."

She nodded, her nerves easing slightly but not completely. "Yeah, it's just... new for me. I'm not sure how I feel about it."

Jamal nodded, his expression friendly and understanding. "I get it. We didn't mean to make you uncomfortable. It's something we're open about, but it's totally okay if it's not something you're interested in."

Sam exhaled, feeling a bit relieved but still flustered. "Thank you. I just don't know if I'm ready for that kind of thing."

Erin smiled reassuringly. "No pressure at all. We totally understand."

As they continued their conversation, the mood shifted back to something lighter but Sam still felt a little uncertain. She knew that this was all about exploring new possibilities but BDSM? That idea left her feeling so out of her depth. She and Mike would have to have a long talk about where their boundaries truly lay.

Eventually, Erin glanced at the time and smiled at Sam and Mike. "This was a lot of fun," she said warmly. "I think we should do this again sometime, no pressure, of course. Just whenever you both feel comfortable

Jamal nodded, giving them a friendly smile. "Yeah, this was a great first step. We'd love to get to know you two even more."

"I think we'd like that," she replied, glancing at Mike for confirmation. He nodded in agreement, a small smile playing on his lips.

By the end of the night, they'd all agreed to meet again. Walking back to the car, Sam felt different emotions. She felt excitement, she felt curiosity and the underlying uncertainty about getting involved with Jamal and Erin.

But at least she was exploring this with Mike. She glanced over at him, squeezing his hand when they reached the car. "Thank you," she said softly. "For being willing to try this."

He squeezed her hand back, a faint smile on his lips. "Anything for you, Sam. Let's see where this takes us."

CHAPTER SIX: The Orgy

Sam found herself oscillating between curiosity to try out this thing with Jamal and hesitation over how it would go.. Jamal had been patient, sensing her reluctance but never pushing her further than she was ready for. Instead, he tried easing her into the idea in his own gentle way.

One day, her phone pinged with a message from Jamal. When she opened it, there was a video, along with a short, reassuring note: 'Nothing intense, just a taste. Let me know what you think.'

Sam hesitated, glancing around to make sure she was alone before pressing play. The video started with a softly lit scene, nothing too intense or overly dramatic. It showed a man and woman, both fully clothed at first, with the woman's wrists gently tied with silk. The man was attentive and careful and he adjusted the ties, checking that she was comfortable. The atmosphere seemed more about trust than anything else. It felt almost artistic, with nothing harsh or aggressive.

As Sam watched, she noticed the subtle way the woman responded to the restraint, her breathing slowing as if she was giving in to the moment. She noticed how the man kept his focus on her, making sure she was okay every step of the way. There was a sense of connection between them, a balance of control and tenderness. It wasn't the harsh image Sam might've had in mind when she first thought about 'BDSM', instead, there was almost an intimacy she hadn't expected.

The video ended with the woman smiling, her head resting on the man's shoulder, and Sam found herself exhaling, feeling oddly turned on.

When her phone pinged again, it was another message from him: 'There's more to it than people think. It's about trust and connection, not just control. But we only do what you're comfortable with.'

Sam found herself smiling a little. She watched the video again, noticing more details. She still felt hesitant but there was no denying that a part of her was curious, maybe even... intrigued.

Then, she got another text from Jamal, this time inviting her to meet him in a hotel. He promised her a safe and comfortable space, assuring her he wouldn't push any boundaries she wasn't ready for. Sam thought about it, her mind going back to the video. This was definitely different from everything she had experienced so far and the thought of experiencing it with Jamal was certainly tempting.

Sam walked into the hotel, her heart racing. As she walked through the lobby, she tried to remind herseld to breathe, to stay calm. She walked over to the receptionist, inquiring about Jamal's room number.

She was directed to his room after they placed a call to him to confirm that he was waiting for someone. When she stepped into the room, she found Jamal waiting for her.

"Hey there," he said, smiling as he stepped forward to greet her. "I'm so glad you came."

He gently took her shoes off, kneeling down in front of her and looking up with those kind eyes. She felt a flutter in her stomach as he moved with care, as if he was treating her like something precious.

"Let's get you comfortable," he said, guiding her to the bed while soft music played in the background.

Sam sat on the edge of the bed. Jamal took her hands, looking into her eyes. "How about a massage? Just to help you relax?"

She nodded, grateful for his thoughtfulness. As he worked on her shoulders, his hands were firm and gentle, kneading away all the tension in her muscles. She let out a soft sigh, feeling herself begin to unwind under his touch.

After a few moments of silence, Sam hesitated, then spoke up. "I just want to say, I'm still worried about the whole BDSM thing. It's so new to me."

Jamal paused, his hands still resting on her back. "I completely understand," he replied softly. "We don't have to dive into that tonight if you're not ready. We can take it slow."

"Really?" she asked, looking back at him.

"Absolutely," he said, a reassuring smile on his face. "You're beautiful just the way you are. I wouldn't need anything else to get off. It's all about making you feel comfortable."

His words sent a wave of warmth through her and she felt a little more at ease. "Thank you. I just..."

"Shh," he interrupted gently, leaning down to place a kiss on her shoulder. "Let's just enjoy this moment."

He continued the massage, his hands moving down her back, loosening her muscles further. Sam closed her eyes, focusing on the sensations, no doubt about it, she felt safe. A complete 180 from how she felt with Tyrell.

After a while, Jamal's hands moved to her waist, slowly sliding around to her front. He leaned in closer, his breath warm against her skin. "How does this feel?"

"Really good," she admitted, feeling her breath hitch a little.

"Good," he murmured, his hands gliding up to her breasts, gently cupping them. The sensation sent shivers through her body. "Just relax. Let me take care of you."

Sam let out a breathy sigh, feeling herself melting into the bed. Jamal was soft handed but there was this subtle possession in it. He leaned over and took her lips into a soft kiss, not the harsh ones she would usually get from the other men she had booked Jo with but a genuine, slow, sweet kiss. And she kissed him back, eagerly.

As their kisses grew more heated, Jamal pulled back slightly, his eyes dark. "I want to try something, okay? Just to ease you into the idea of kink."

Her heart raced at the thought but she felt curious, too. "What do you mean?"

He smiled, reaching for a soft scarf that lay on the bedside table. "I'd like to tie your arms back a little. Just to see how it feels. I promise it won't be anything crazy."

Sam's breath caught in her throat, her hesitation creeping back. But looking into his eyes, she could see the sincerity there. "Okay," she said, though her voice trembled slightly.

Jamal took the scarf and gently wrapped it around her wrists, securing them to the headboard of the bed. "How's that?" he asked, checking in on her.

"Not too tight," she replied, surprised at how secure it felt without being uncomfortable.

"Perfect," he said, his smile returning. He leaned in again, kissing her softly before trailing his lips down her neck. Sam shivered at his touch, the anticipation swirling in her stomach.

Then, Jamal reached for a small vibrator that had been lying on the bedside table. "I want to add this into the mix. Just to heighten the pleasure a bit."

"What do I do?" Sam asked, excitement and nervousness bubbling inside her.

"Just let go," he said, turning it on and placing it against her sensitive skin. The vibrations sent wave after wave of pleasurable sensations through her body, causing her to gasp.

When did she become so sensitive?

"Oh..." Sam gasped, her body arching towards him, instinctively craving more.

"Just like that," he encouraged, watching her reaction. "Let me know what feels good."

He continued to kiss her, moving lower, his lips tracing a path down her body. The combination of the vibrations and his mouth on her skin sent her mind spinning. She felt exhilarated and also strangely vulnerable, a strange mix that terrified and thrilled her.

"Jamal..." she breathed, her voice shaky but he only smiled against her skin, focusing on her pleasure.

Just when it felt like she was about to let go, Jamal began giving her light spanks on the side of her body as she changed the speed from the vibrator. He was testing her limits while still keeping it light.

"Does that feel good?" he asked.

"Yes," she gasped, her body responding to every touch, every kiss, every playful smack.

Jamal continued to play with her boundaries, making it clear that he has no plans of penetrating her. His whole plan here was to get her to calm down and see that there was nothing scary about BDSM.

And it looked like his plan was working.

Just as quickly as he started this session, he ended it. Sam looked at him with glazed eyes, wondering why he stopped.

He smiled shyly and said, "If I went any further, I might have to do something I wasn't planning on doing tonight."

He gave a pointed look downward and Sam's eyes opened in shock when she saw the massive tent pitched in his pants. Had she done that to him? Driven him to this point of excruciating pleasure. She could see it throbbing already.

"I hope you'll give me another chance to do this. I would really like to fuck you next time." He whispered, leaning down and giving her a slight kiss.

Jamal had shown Sam a different side of intimacy and she couldn't shake the smile off her face as she left the hotel, her heart still racing from the experience.

Later that evening, she found herself sitting on the couch with Mike, who was catching up on some sports highlights. He glanced over at her, noticing the way she was practically glowing. "You seem happy. Did you have a good time today?" he asked.

"I did," Sam admitted, her cheeks warming at the thought of Jamal. "Really good, actually."

Mike raised an eyebrow, intrigued. "Good to hear. Are you feeling ready to... explore more with him?"

Just then, her phone buzzed, interrupting their conversation. It was a message from Jamal: "Hey, how about you and Mike come over tonight? We can chill and discuss our new dynamic. It'll be fun!"

Sam felt a rush of excitement at the idea. "Jamal wants us to come over tonight," she said, biting her lip.

"Sounds like a good idea," Mike replied. "You enjoyed your time with him, right?"

"Definitely," she said, nodding vigorously. "He really helped me feel more comfortable."

"Then let's go," Mike said with a nod. "I trust you, and it'll be nice to see how we can make this work together."

The atmosphere in Jamal's apartment was calm. When they knocked, Jamal welcomed them with open arms, his charm radiating as he greeted them both.

"Glad you could make it!" he said, his smile infectious. "I thought we could start with some drinks and just hang out for a bit."

They settled into the cozy living room, drinks in hand, as the conversation flowed easily. Jamal was watching Sam intently as she sipped on her drink and she didn't know whether to feel uncomfortable or flattered.

After a while, Jamal leaned back, a thoughtful expression on his face. "You know, I really enjoyed our last session, Sam. You have such incredible body."

"Thanks," she said, her cheeks warming at the compliment. "I really appreciate how patient you've been with me."

He smiled, leaning in closer. "It's easy when you're so receptive. And I think there's more we can explore together."

Mike, sitting beside Sam, watched the exchange. "What do you have in mind?" he asked, leaning forward slightly, clearly interested in where this was heading.

Jamal's gaze flicked between them, "Well, we can start with something simple. Just some light teasing, a little playfulness. I think Sam would enjoy it."

"What do you mean?" Sam asked.

Jamal smiled, his voice low and inviting. "Let's have some fun. How about a little game? I want to see how well I can push your limits, Sam. With Mike's permission, of course."

Mike nodded, clearly intrigued. "I'm open to seeing where this goes."

With that encouragement, Jamal stood up, extending his hand to Sam. "Come on, let's move to the bedroom. It'll be more comfortable there."

Sam took his hand, her pulse quickening as she followed him into the bedroom. He led her to the bed then made her sit in it, after which he turned to face her.

"Let's start with something simple," he said. "Just lie back and relax. I want to see how you respond to a little teasing."

He leaned down, brushing his lips softly against her skin, and Sam felt a thrill run through her.

"You're so sensitive Sam, I love it. Just focus on the sensations," he instructed. "Let everything else fade away."

He began to kiss her neck, moving down her collarbone. She closed her eyes, surrendering to the moment as Jamal explored her body, his kisses trailing lower.

"Sam, you can tell me to stop at any time," he murmured, flicking his tongue down the indent in her collarbone. "But I want to see how far we can take this."

Just then, Mike walked in, watching the scene unfold. Sam glanced over at him, her heart racing as she realized he was fully aware of what was happening.

Jamal paused for a moment, locking eyes with Mike. "Is this okay with you?" he asked, ensuring they were both on the same page.

Mike nodded, his expression filled with a hint of desire. "Yeah, I'm good with it," he replied, leaning against the doorframe.

Encouraged by Mike's approval, Jamal turned his attention back to Sam, a wicked grin on his face. "Let's kick it up a notch, shall we?"

With that, he grabbed the scarf he had used before, gently binding her wrists again. Sam felt a thrill at the idea of being restrained, her heart racing as Jamal took control.

"Just relax and enjoy," he said, teasing her lips with his. "I promise you'll love this."

Mike watched intently as Jamal tied his wife's wrist to the headboard then knelt in between her thighs, opening them up for him. Slowly, Jamal's hand went up and down Sam's thigh, squeezing, pinching, sending different sensations through her, causing her to make a variety of sounds.

Jamal chuckled to himself, "This would be so much better if you were blindfolded." He turned to Mike then pointed to the dresser next to the bed, "Could you get the blindfold out of there, please? Don't just stand there and watch."

Mike blinked, like he was surprised he was suddenly a part of this now but he walked over to the dresser and took out the blindfold. He handed it to Jamal but he shook his head.

"Put it on her, put the blindfold on your wife Mike." Jamal said, his voice dangerously low.

Mike obeyed and knelt on the bed by Sam's head, slipping the blindfold on her. He turned to Jamal, who was smiling by this point.

"Now you get to watch me take your wife." he whispered, settling himself between Sam's thighs then burying his face in them. Sam buckled instantly, feeling his warm, wet tongue stroke the tip of her clit. Jamal wasn't aggressive about it or anything, he was slow and gentle like he was savoring the taste of her.

Sam tugged at the restraints her wrists were in, wanting to grab onto Jamal's head because of how overwhelming the sensations he was giving her was. Jamal's tongue circled and flicked against the head of her clit, making a sucking motion at the same time.

While he did that, he brought his finger over and slipped one then two into her. He moved his finger within her, earning moans from her. Sam began to buck her hips against his fingers, trying her hardest to cum against them.

Jamal came up for air, his mouth glistening from Sam's juices. "You should join us Mike, I think Sam would like to give you a blowjob. Isn't that right Sam?"

Mike looked over at Sam, wondering if that was what she really wanted but she looked so flushed and breathless that he wasn't sure she would even be able to speak.

Still though, he unbuckled his pants and revealed his boner, one that had come on from watching Jamal eat his wife out. He pressed his dick into her mouth and she opened up for him, causing him to moan as the head of his dick got enveloped by her mouth.

Sam moaned and tried to bob her head as best as she could, up and down the shaft. Jamal watched them go at it for a while before burying his face back into Sam's thighs, lapping at her clit once again.

Erin came in at that moment and stood by the doorframe, watching them intently. Mike was shoving his penis down Sam's throat while her husband licked her up and tried to make her cum with his fingers.

The sight turned her on.

Careful not to alert them to her presence, she walked over to the closet across the bed and took out a purple vibrator before walking over to a nearby chair where she could watch all three of them go at it.

She took off her shorts, spread her legs then brought the vibrator to her clit, turning it on. The vibration instantly caused her to throw her head back as shock waves went through her body.

The sound of the vibrator drew Mike's attention and he watched as Erin threw her head back, covering her mouth with one hand whilst the other held the vibrator she used to pleasure herself. If he was hard before then he was even harder now, unable to take his eyes off her as she moved her hips against the vibrator.

Sam, at that moment, was reaching the edge. She was so overcome by what Jamal was doing to her that she had no choice but to let go. Jamal used his thumb to circle her clit which caused her to finally lose control, and she let out a strained moan even as Mike's dick was in her mouth.

Jamal got back on his knees and looked at Sam, whose head was rolled back, no longer pleasuring Mike. He turned to the direction of where the vibration was coming from and saw his wife right in the thick of getting herself off. At that moment he got a sneaky idea.

He undid Sam's restraints, turning her on her stomach with the intention of taking her from behind. Meanwhile he felt his wife could not miss out on the fun so he asked Mike to join her so the both of them could watch him and Sam go at it.

Sam was out of breath but not enough to miss out on the chance to fuck Jamal. He gave her a light smack on her asss then propped her up on her knees so she was arching in front of him, her ass and pussy in full view.

"Gosh, I want to bury my face in there again." He said, as he brought his dick up to her entrance for the first time. "But I'm going to savor this even more."

Jamal groaned as he slid into Sam slowly. She winced as she was extra sensitive down there but she started to moan when he moved within her, savoring the way her walls drew him in.

"Fuckkk," he whispered as he thrusted into Sam repeatedly. He gripped onto her hips as hard as he could and watched as each slap from his body caused hers to jiggle. He wanted to go deeper, harder, faster but he knew he had to pace himself.

By this time, Mike was besides Erin, stroking himself whilst she got herself off with the vibrator. She put the vibrator down then looked at Mike as he stroked himself while he watched Jamal fuck his wife.

"You know what's even better than a vibrator?" she said all of a sudden, drawing Mike's attention away from the other two.

"What?" Mike asked.

"Real dick." she said, as she tipped her finger to summon him over to her. Under normal circumstances, Mike would hesitate but he couldn't at this point not when he was so horny.

Without wasting any time, he was in front of Erin and within her in a moment, slapping into her hard and reckless, nothing like the refined strokes from Jamal. Erin didn't seem to care though, she held onto Mike and moaned out loud as he drove himself into her.

The smacking from their bodies drew Jamal's attention and he smirked when he realized that his plan had worked after all. Jamal made his thrusts more intense, not to be outmatched by the erratic thrusts from Mike.

He leaned over and pounded into Sam repeatedly, she was so wet and so
warm, the sound of all the bodies slapping into each other was driving him crazy. Just as he felt like he was about to lose control, he heard groans coming from the corner and out of the corner of his eye, he saw Mike and Erin cumming together.

That was enough to get him where he wanted to go and he groaned deeply as he gave two more really intense thrusts before pulling out and cumming all over the sheets.

He tried to catch his breath as the spasms faded away then smacked Sam's ass again just for the fun of it before collapsing on the bed, out of breath.

"I gotta say, you white people know how to wear a guy out." he said, chuckling.

All four of them crawled into bed and before either knew what was happening, they were fast asleep, exhausted from the sex and the orgasms.

THE END

Dear reader,

Thank you for completing this series! Do you want more? Check out my *Submitting to the Dominatrix* Series.

Exclusive erotic short story club

Want even more? You can join my exclusive erotic short club **for free**. By doing so, you will get a bunch of free stories (before I publish them on Amazon), audiobook coupon codes, and much more! Join here: https://bit.ly/3WJsqRp

Or email me at amber.carden.books@gmail.com and I will send you a link!

Amber

© Copyright 2024 - All rights reserved.

The content contained within this book may not be reproduced, duplicated, or transmitted without direct written permission from the author or the publisher.

This book is copyright protected. It is only for personal use. You cannot amend, distribute, sell, use, quote or paraphrase any part, or the content within this book, without the consent of the author or publisher.

www.ingramcontent.com/pod-product-compliance
Lightning Source LLC
LaVergne TN
LVHW041632070526
838199LV00052B/3322